An Island in the Sun

written by Stella Blackstone
illustrated by Nicoletta Ceccoli

Barefoot Books
Celebrating Art and Story

I spy with my little eye a bird flying by.

I spy with my little eye the sun in the sky and a bird flying by.

I spy with my little eye a dolphin jumping free and the sun in the sky and a bird flying by.

I spy with my little eye an island far from me and a dolphin jumping free

and the sun in the sky and a bird flying by.

I spy with my little eye a big tangly tree on an island far from me

and a dolphin jumping free and the sun in the sky and a bird flying by.

I spy with my little eye a beach beside the sea and a big tangly tree on an island far from me and a dolphin jumping free and the sun in the sky and a bird flying by.

I spy with my little eye someone waiting for me on a beach beside the sea

and a big tangly tree on an island close to me and a dolphin jumping free

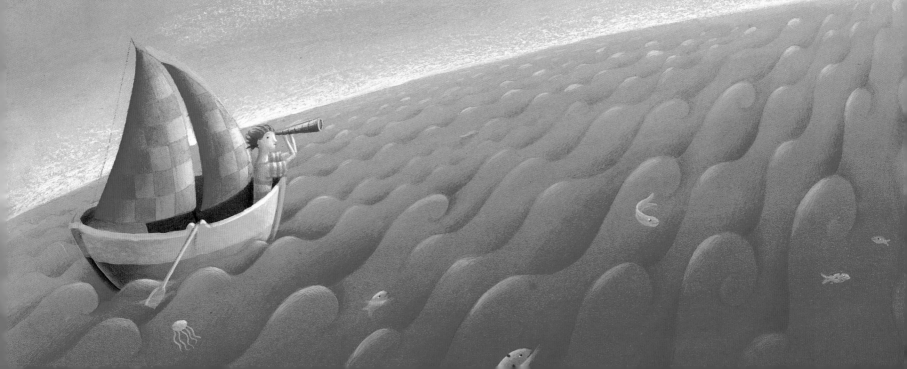

and the sun in the sky and a bird flying by.

Together we laugh, together we play, together we fish 'til the end of the day.

What did I spy with my little eye?

And shall we sail home now, just you and I?

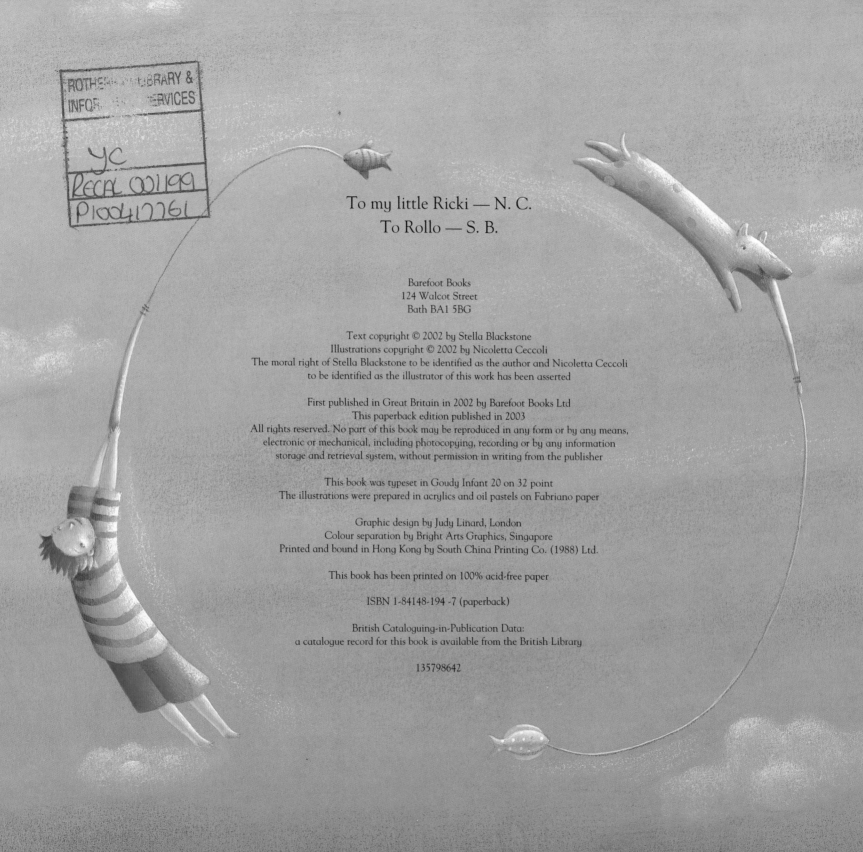

To my little Ricki — N. C.
To Rollo — S. B.

Barefoot Books
124 Walcot Street
Bath BA1 5BG

This book was typeset in Goudy Infant 20 on 32 point
The illustrations were prepared in acrylics and oil pastels on Fabriano paper

Graphic design by Judy Linard, London
Colour separation by Bright Arts Graphics, Singapore
Printed and bound in Hong Kong by South China Printing Co. (1988) Ltd.

This book has been printed on 100% acid-free paper

ISBN 1-84148-194 -7 (paperback)

British Cataloguing-in-Publication Data:
a catalogue record for this book is available from the British Library

135798642